Kitty

Humbug

is   a

Poodle   Cat

Kitty Humbug™

Published in 2009 by Madaras Gallery Inc. 1535 E. Broadway, Tucson, AZ 85719. Printed in the United States.

www.madaras.com

First U.S. Edition 2009

Library of Congress Cataloging-In-Publication Data

ISBN 978-1-892344-56-4

Special Thanks to: Sandy Levine, Sandra Levine Productions; Caroline L. Fairhurst; Miroslaw Tymosiak; and Dr. Richard Panzero, Starsky, and the River Road Pet Clinic Staff.

Dedicated to the memory of Klondike "Kitty Angel" Madaras

Kitty Humbug's Christmas Tail

Written by Diana Madaras
Illustrated by Diana Madaras & Ric Nielsen

Kitty Humbug's Christmas Tail

On Christmas Eve, Santa guided his reindeer across the night sky, pulling a sleigh full of presents for the children of the world. The packages were wrapped in beautiful paper of every color—silver and green and gold and blue—each tied with a pretty red ribbon on top. Santa's path was lit by one trillion bright stars twinkling in the night. But one star just above the sleigh kept getting bigger and bigger and brighter and brighter.

"Look," said the reindeer Tuffy as he pointed above his ear. "The star is falling from the sky and it's going to hit us in the head. Go faster, Blazer," he yelled to the lead reindeer. "Go faster!"

"I'm going as fast as I can!" cried Blazer just as the star fell straight down and nicked the side of the sleigh with a loud thump. The sleigh tipped to the side and all the presents slid to the very edge. The reindeers' hooves scrambled as fast as they could and finally the sleigh was saved from turning over.

"Wow, that was close!" exclaimed Tuffy, out of breath. Just then Santa groaned loudly.

"My dear reindeer, I'm afraid we have a problem," Santa said, doubling over in pain. "I fear my arm is broken. The star hit my elbow when it crashed down beside us."

The reindeer all gasped. "My goodness!" cried reindeer Max. "What will we do? We must get Santa to the hospital to fix his arm!"

"I don't know where the hospital is," Blazer said.

"I have an idea," said Tuffy in his very deep reindeer voice. "We can take Santa to the animal hospital where Dr. Pea fixed my sore hoof last Christmas. If he can fix my hoof, surely he can fix Santa's arm. Then we can get back to delivering presents to the children."

"Good thinking," Santa said. "Hurry then to the animal hospital. We've got work to do!"

The reindeer looked down upon the earth and spied the animal hospital. Blazer guided the sleigh to a gentle landing on the roof. He stamped his hoof impatiently, hoping the noise would wake Dr. Pea.

But to the reindeers' surprise, when the squeaky old door to the hospital opened it was not Dr. Pea at all, but rather a cat. And a funny-looking cat, at that, with a head like a lion, a body like a poodle, and crazy blue eyes that squinted under the porch lights.

The cat looked angry and mean as he shouted at the reindeer in a gruff, scratchy voice, "Who goes there? Who dares to wake Kitty Humbug from his nightly slumber?"

Blazer peered over the side of the roof and said, "We're the reindeer from the North Pole and Santa has been injured. We need Dr. Pea's help."

"Santa's reindeer has a red nose, not a silly blue one!" Humbug said. "Even I know that."

"You're thinking of my dad," Blazer said. "He retired last year. My nose used to be red, but when I was a baby I got frostbite and it turned blue."

"Whatever," the kitty exclaimed as he slammed the door shut and shuffled back down the hall to his warm, fuzzy bed.

Blazer jumped back with surprise. "What's wrong with that grumpy cat?"

"Maybe he doesn't know who Santa is," said Max.

"Oh, hogwash," said Tuffy. "Everyone knows Santa. This humbug cat is just an old grouch. Let's all stomp our feet on the roof and we'll MAKE him open the door."

The reindeer jumped up and down and caused such a clatter that Kitty Humbug fell right out of his bed. He rolled on the floor and held his paws to his ears, but the noise would not stop. Finally, he marched back down the hall and threw open the door once again.

"Go away, you noisy reindeer!" Humbug shouted as he shook his paw at the roof. "Go back to the North Pole and leave me alone! You're upsetting all my sick animals. Don't you know this is a hospital?"

Blazer leaned over the roof and shouted sternly, "Listen to me, you grumpy old cat. Dr. Pea has got to fix Santa's arm so he can slide down the chimneys tonight. It's Christmas Eve! Don't you know? Children all over the world will be so sad if Christmas doesn't come."

"Christmas, smishmas," said Kitty Humbug. "And I don't like children, anyway. They are mean! When I was little, they pulled my fur and yanked my tail. At night, they put me out on the doorstep with no food or blanket. When I grew up, they didn't want me anymore and sent me to live at a scary place for kitties with no families. Tell Santa I'm busy. Come back tomorrow and then I'll see about fetching Dr. Pea."

"Tomorrow is too late," Blazer insisted. "Santa needs help now! Where is Dr. Pea anyway?"

"He lives next door and I'm sure he's sound asleep," Humbug huffed.

"Then wake him," Blazer demanded, "or we'll stomp on your roof all night long!"

The reindeer jumped up and down again and made as much noise as they could. Kitty Humbug raised his paw to the roof and yelled, "STOP. STOP. I can't take it anymore. I hate noise! I'll go wake Dr. Pea. Just stop that awful noise!"

Kitty Humbug grabbed his bathrobe and hurried off into the night. Ten minutes later he returned with the good doctor at his heels.

"Is it true Santa is on the roof?" Dr. Pea looked up in amazement to see the sleigh and eight reindeer.

Blazer nodded his bright blue nose yes.

"I'll get a ladder and help Santa down," said Dr. Pea. "Humbug, go check on the animals in the hospital and calm them down. I can hear them barking and meowing from here."

Kitty Humbug walked back into the hospital and told each dog, cat and bird about the reindeer on the roof and Santa's broken arm. He comforted them one by one and assured them everything was all right. After all, that was Humbug's job. He had promised to work hard after Dr. Pea had rescued him from the shelter for homeless kitties five years ago.

So on this very unusual Christmas Eve, Humbug's last stop was Kitty Klondike's room. Humbug used to be angry that the white kitty was so much work, but he grew to love and admire his little friend who never once complained, though his life was so hard. And the kitty was white, just like Humbug, and he liked that, too. Sometimes he would pretend the cat was his long-lost brother since Humbug had no family or children to love him.

Loud noises scared Kitty Klondike because he could not run away from danger. Klondike was so sick he could not even walk or eat by himself. He needed Humbug's help for everything. "What happened up there on the roof?" Kitty Klondike asked softly.

Kitty Humbug cradled his best friend in his arms because the little white cat had been startled by all the clatter.

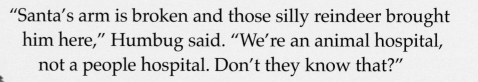

"Santa's arm is broken and those silly reindeer brought him here," Humbug said. "We're an animal hospital, not a people hospital. Don't they know that?"

"I'm sure Dr. Pea will help Santa the best he can," Kitty Klondike said.

"I'm going to put you back in your bed," Humbug said, "and see what's going on with Santa. I'll come back later to tuck you in like I do every night."

"OK," Kitty Klondike smiled softly. "I'll be right here waiting for you."

Klondike was always so patient and kind with everyone, Humbug thought. When the other animals made fun of him because he could not walk, the little kitty would just smile and say nice words even to the meanest of them.

Humbug stroked Klondike's head then trotted into the exam room as Dr. Pea finished bandaging Santa's arm.

"This will do for now, Santa," said Dr. Pea. "But I'll have to drive you to the people hospital. You'll need a cast for that broken arm and that could take all night, you know."

"But it's Christmas!" Santa exclaimed with dismay. "What about the children? No presents for the children? I cannot let that happen!" Santa stood up quickly, but grabbed his arm in pain and sank back onto the table.

13

"I'm sorry, Santa," Dr. Pea said. "You won't be sliding down any chimneys tonight."

Word spread quickly throughout the animal hospital that for the first time ever there would be no Christmas presents for the children. All the animals hung their heads thinking about how sad their human families would be when they learned that Santa had not come.

The reindeer on the roof heard the news, too. "No Christmas!" cried Blazer. "This cannot be."

"We have to find a way to get the presents to the children," Max said. "Can't we find someone who can drive the sleigh?"

"Dr. Pea can't do it," Blazer said. "He has to take Santa to the hospital."

"Even if we could find someone," Tuffy said with his head hung low, "no one could get down the chimney like Santa. We'd need a miracle."

"Wait!" Blazer raised his head high and shouted. "I know someone who can do it, but it's not going to be easy to convince him." He smiled a mischievous reindeer grin.

The other reindeer looked at each other, puzzled. "Who in the world could drive the sleigh and get up and down the chimneys?" they asked shaking their heads.

"How about a grumpy old cat we all know?" said Blazer.

"Oh no! Not Kitty Humbug?" the reindeer shouted in unison.

"Yes, Kitty Humbug," Blazer beamed. "He's our only hope. Dr. Pea has to drive Santa to the hospital and the rest of the animals here are sick. There's nobody else. We can help Humbug guide the sleigh and he can use his claws to climb up and down the chimney."

"But even if we help him guide the sleigh," Max said, "he won't do it. He doesn't care about Christmas or the children."

"I know how we can get him to do it," Blazer smiled so big all his white reindeer teeth showed.

The reindeer looked at one another, nodded their heads and then jumped up and down on the roof so hard it almost cracked.

Humbug stormed out the front door once again. "What's wrong with you reindeer?"

Blazer Blue Nose ™

15

"Humbug, we want you to drive the sleigh tonight," Max said, batting his big green eyes.

"We want you to deliver the presents, man," Tuffy chimed in.

"Yes, Humbug," Blazer said quietly, his blue nose beaming in the night. "We want *you* to save Christmas."

"Save Christmas, my fur!" Humbug shouted back. "That's Santa's job, not mine. I don't know how to drive your silly old sleigh anyway. I'm going back to bed. I need my beauty rest."

"Beauty rest? Ha!" chuckled Tuffy. "You're the funniest looking lion-poodle-cat I've ever seen."

Max added, "And a mean little critter, too. How could you let down all the children of the world?"

"Like this," Humbug said as he slammed the front door behind him and strutted back inside the hospital.

The reindeer all shouted together, "Humbug! Humbug! Humbug! Humbug!"

Humbug held his paws over his ears and tried not to listen to the racket outside. How he hated loud noises!

"Humbug! Humbug! Humbug! Humbug!" the reindeer shouted over and over.

Humbug ran down to Kitty Klondike's room and lifted the little white cat from his bed.

"Those reindeer are driving me batty," grumbled Humbug as he poured warm milk into a small bowl for Kitty Klondike. "Maybe they will lose their voices soon from all that wicked shouting."

"Humbug! Humbug! Humbug! Humbug!" the reindeer kept yelling.

Humbug tried to ignore the noise while he rocked the little white cat in his arms. He raised the bowl of milk to Kitty Klondike's lips but the cat refused to drink.

"What's wrong, Klondike?" Humbug asked. "Warm milk is your favorite!"

Kitty Klondike didn't utter a sound.

"Klondike, are you OK?" Humbug grew alarmed.

"Kitty Klondike, talk to me," Humbug pleaded. "What's wrong with you tonight?"

Humbug looked into the eyes of his little white friend and saw that the cat was terribly sick. And now his friend was crying. He had never seen Kitty Klondike cry before.

"Why are you crying, Klondike?" Humbug asked.

Kitty Klondike looked up at his friend and said, "I'm crying for the children, Humbug. My heart is breaking because the children will be so sad tomorrow. I'm crying because for the first time ever, Santa will not come. If only my paws worked, I would drive the sleigh myself. You know what it's like to be sad, don't you Humbug?"

Humbug nodded yes.

"Well, children can be sad, too, just like you."

One huge tear as big as a puddle rolled down Kitty Klondike's face and landed right on Humbug's chest. As the tear soaked through Humbug's fur and touched his heart, he suddenly felt the sadness of all the children of the world because there would be no Christmas. It reminded him of how he felt when he was sent to the shelter for kitties with no families.

He could also feel the pain that Kitty Klondike knew every day from his illness. He now understood how very brave his little friend was never to complain. Even tonight, when Klondike was so sick, he did not cry for himself but only for the children.

And with that single tear, the hard heart of the grumpy lion-poodle-cat named Humbug melted like a snowball in the afternoon sun.

Kitty Klondike looked up at his friend and smiled. "You've found your heart again, Humbug, and the reindeer will help you guide the sleigh. But it's your choice, my friend. Whatever happens this Christmas, it's all up to you."

Humbug gently placed Kitty Klondike on his bed and covered him with a blanket. He stood quietly for a moment tugging at the scruffy white fur beneath his chin. Suddenly Humbug proclaimed, "There's no time to waste, Klondike. I'm going to do it. I'm going to save Christmas! I'm sorry to leave you right now, but there's work to be done. I see I have been an old fool. I'm sure there are many, many wonderful children who deserve a merry Christmas. You've taught me so much, my little friend. You are an angel to me and I love you, Kitty Klondike."

"I love you, too, Humbug."

"You do?" Humbug's eyes grew huge.

"Yes, very much," Kitty Klondike said. "In your heart, you know it."

Humbug dropped his chin to his chest and he squeezed his eyes shut. No one had ever told him they loved him. Humbug's crazy blue eyes filled with water and the grumpy old cat cried like a baby kitten.

Brushing the tears away, he touched Klondike's face, then hurried down the hall to his closet. He fetched the Santa suit Dr. Pea made him wear at the Christmas party every year, squeezed into it and climbed up to the roof.

"OK, OK, you noisy beasts. I **will** drive your sleigh tonight," Humbug said. He quickly added, "but I'm not doing it for you. I'm doing it for Kitty Klondike. He has shown me what Christmas really means through his kindness throughout the year, not just on this night."

The reindeer shouted with joy as Humbug jumped into Santa's seat and swooshed his poodle tail in the air. All the animals from the hospital ran into the parking lot to watch. They carried Kitty Klondike out on a blanket so he could watch, too.

"Wait!" Humbug stood up suddenly and held his paw high in the air just before the sleigh took off. "There's one more thing to do."

Humbug gazed down upon all the animals in the parking lot below him.

"Kitty Klondike," he called softly, "would you like to ride with me on the sleigh tonight?"

Klondike sat up on the blanket of towels, perked up his ears and smiled with joy. "Oh, Humbug. I would love that! It will be my best Christmas ever."

The animals picked up the blanket and carried Klondike up the ladder onto the roof.

With Klondike nestled in one arm, Humbug then commanded, "All right now, you rowdy reindeer. Show me what you've got!"

Blazer's blue nose lit up brightly as he turned his head back to signal the other reindeer. He nodded once to the animals below and in an instant the sleigh flew off Dr. Pea's roof into the night of one trillion twinkling stars.

The only sound that could be heard outside the animal hospital as the sleigh took off was a faint chant from the reindeer that sounded something like, "Humbug! Humbug! Humbug! Humbug!"

And for the first time ever, the animals saw the grumpy old cat named Humbug smile as the sleigh raced out of sight. Some say they even saw a little twinkle in his crazy blue eyes.

Diana Madaras is an award-winning artist who is as equally well known for her bold, colorful artwork as she is for her generous charitable giving. Madaras owns two galleries in Tucson, Arizona, that feature her work exclusively. She is the president of Art for Animals, a foundation she started in 1999 that helps abused, injured and orphaned animals. Part of the proceeds from all Kitty Humbug products will fund Art for Animals projects. *Kitty Humbug's Christmas Tail* is Madaras' first book; it is dedicated to the memory of her beloved handicapped cat, Klondike.

Ric Nielsen has been the art director for the City of Tucson for 29 years. He was awarded the bronze medal for animation at the International Film and Television Festival of New York, and also has won Addy Awards for graphic design on both the local and national levels. Nielsen and Madaras have worked together on art projects for more than 20 years. "Kitty Humbug was one of the most fun and challenging projects I've ever done," Nielsen said. He is a graduate of the University of Arizona and is married with five children.

Much More Kitty Humbug™
See the real life Humbug in the video
Sample the song "Kitty Humbug the Cat"
Find all Kitty Humbug products at **www.madaras.com**